Don't Believe It!

Fibs and Facts About Animals

by Melvin Berger

illustrated by Bryn Barnard

SCHOLASTIC INC.

New York   Toronto   London   Auckland   Sydney

For Matty, with love from his Zayde
—M.B.

For my father, who taught me to be skeptical
—B.B.

ISBN 0-590-68852-9

Text copyright © 1997 by Melvin Berger.
Illustrations copyright © 1997 by Scholastic Inc.
All rights reserved. Published by Scholastic Inc.

12 11 10 9 8 7 6 5 4 3 2 1   6 7 8 9/9 0 1/0

Printed in the U.S.A.   24
First Scholastic printing, April 1997

CONTENTS

Birds and Bats
4

About Bugs
12

The Barnyard Bunch
17

Big and Wild
24

Small and Wild
35

Carnival of Cats
42

Creepers and Crawlers
49

Fishy Facts
59

Birds and Bats

An ostrich hides its head in the sand.

DON'T BELIEVE IT!

Usually an ostrich doesn't have to hide. It's the largest living bird. It can be up to eight feet tall. Most ostriches weigh over 300 pounds. An ostrich can knock over a large animal with one kick of its powerful legs. And it can run up to 40 miles an hour.

But sometimes an ostrich does try to hide. It lowers its head and neck flat on the ground. People think the ostrich is putting its head in the sand. Really it is not. The bird is just holding its head *on* the sand.

The bald eagle has no head feathers.
DON'T BELIEVE IT!

 The large, powerful bald eagle is the national bird of the United States. But it is not really bald. It has white feathers on its head. So why is it called the *bald* eagle?

The English settlers gave the bird its name. They had not seen this kind of bird in England. In those days *bald* meant "covered with white fur or feathers." Today bald means without fur, feathers—or hair. But we still call the bird a *bald* eagle.

Birds stay away from scarecrows because they look like people.

DON'T BELIEVE IT!

 Farmers put scarecrows in their fields to scare away crows and other birds. Often they make the scarecrow out of old clothes. The farmers hang the clothes on poles to look like a person.

Have you ever wondered why birds stay away from scarecrows? Is it the shape of the scarecrows? No. Is it the way the wind blows the scarecrows' clothes? No.

Birds keep away because the old clothes *smell* like humans! When the smell wears off, the birds are no longer afraid of the scarecrow.

All penguins live near the South Pole.
DON'T BELIEVE IT!

 Most penguins do live in Antarctica, near the South Pole. But not all penguins do. Penguins can also be found in other parts of the world.

Galapagos
GALAPAGOS ISLANDS

King
ANTARCTIC

Gentoo
SUB-ANTARCTIC

Humbolt
CHILE AND PERU

Magellanic
ATLANTIC AND PACIFIC COASTS OF SOUTH AMERICA

Chinstrap
ANTARCTIC

Rockhopper
ANTARCTIC

Emperor
CONTINENTAL ANTARCTICA

Altogether there are 18 different kinds of penguins. Only two kinds make their home around the South Pole. Others live in New Zealand, Australia, and South Africa. Penguins are even found on the Galapagos Islands. These islands are near the equator. But the waters here are almost as cold as the waters in Antarctica.

Fiordland-Crested
SOUTHERN NEW ZEALAND

Little
SOUTHERN AUSTRALIA
TASMANIA
NEW ZEALAND

Jackass
SOUTHERN AFRICA

Erect-Crested
ANTARCTIC NEW ZEALAND

Royal
SOUTHERN NEW ZEALAND

Adelie
CONTINENTAL ANTARCTICA

Macaroni
SOUTHERN OCEANS

White-Flippered
SOUTH ISLAND NEW ZEALAND

Yellow-Eyed
SOUTH ISLAND NEW ZEALAND

Snares Island
SNARES ISLAND

9

Bats are blind.
DON'T BELIEVE IT!

 Bats zigzag as they fly in the night sky. Some people think bats can't see where they're going. This has led to the saying that anyone who has trouble seeing is "blind as a bat."

But bats are not blind at all. They see very well. Scientists say that bats see as well as humans—perhaps even better.

Some kinds of bats feed on fruits or flowers. They have large eyes and excellent vision. These bats can easily spot their food in the dark.

Many other kinds of bats feed on insects. These bats make high-pitched squeaking sounds as they fly. At the same time they listen for the echoes of their sounds. An echo that bounces back quickly tells them an insect is nearby. They swoop this way and that in the chase. One bat can catch up to 1,000 insects in an hour!

Vampire bats suck blood.
DON'T BELIEVE IT!

Vampire bats are real animals that live in Central and South America. But don't mix them up with vampires—the make-believe creatures that exist only in books and movies. Vampires are supposed to suck human blood.

Vampire bats are small, only about three inches long. They drink blood. But they do not suck blood.

A vampire bat lands on a sleeping person or on an animal. The bat has two teeth that are as sharp as razors. With these teeth it makes a tiny cut in the skin. The cut starts to bleed. The vampire bat then licks up the blood. It looks like a tiny kitten lapping up milk from a dish.

About Bugs

Bees collect honey.
DON'T BELIEVE IT!

 You've probably seen bees flying from flower to flower. And you know that bees make honey. So you may think, "Bees collect honey." Not so! Bees collect *nectar*.

Nectar is a sweet liquid found inside many flowers. The bees suck up the nectar. Each bee has a special stomach where it stores the nectar. When they fly back to the hive, they spit up the nectar. Other bees in the hive add chemicals. This changes the nectar into honey. And the bees then use the honey as food.

Buzibee
NATURAL
HONEY
U.S. GRADE A FANCY
NET WT.
2.2 lbs (1 kg)

Nutrition Facts
Serving Size 1 Tbsp (21g)
Servings 25. Amount per serving. Calories 60. Calories from Fat 0.
Sodium 0mg (0% DV). Total Carb. 17g (6% DV). Sugars 16g. Protein 0g.
0% DV. Percent Daily Values (DV) Are Based On A 2,000 Calorie Diet.

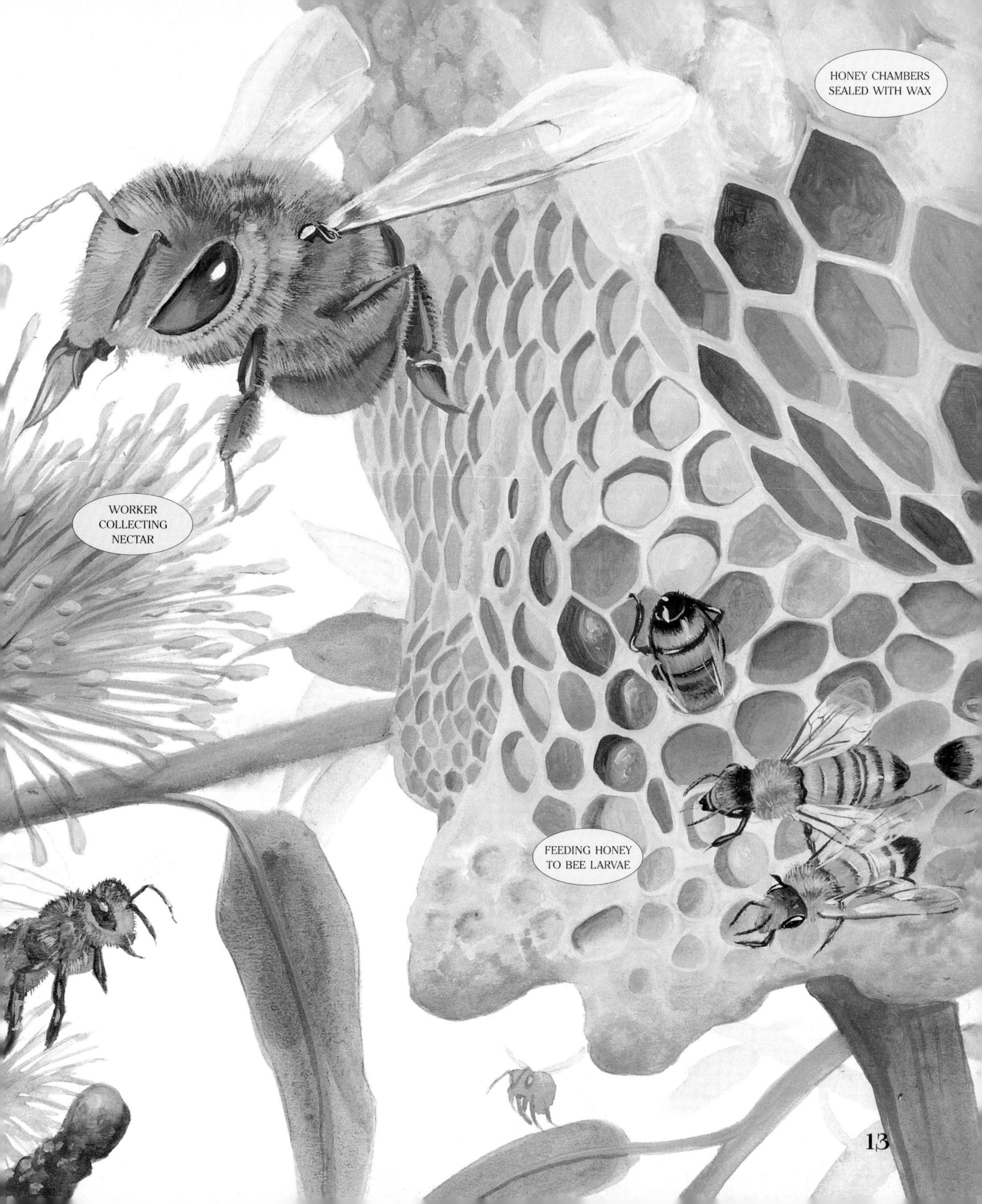

HONEY CHAMBERS SEALED WITH WAX
WORKER COLLECTING NECTAR
FEEDING HONEY TO BEE LARVAE

Monarch butterflies fly south in the fall and north in the spring.

DON'T BELIEVE IT!

Every fall millions of monarch butterflies leave the northern United States and Canada. They fly thousands of miles south to Mexico, Florida, and California. And every spring millions of monarch butterflies head north. It looks as though the butterflies are coming back. But there's a catch. The monarchs that return are not the same ones that left in the fall!

One group of butterflies makes the trip south. They stay there for the winter. On the way back the females lay their eggs. Soon after that, all the adult butterflies die. The eggs, however, hatch and grow into butterflies. The newborns finish the trip back north for the summer.

BUTTERFLY

CHRYSALIS

CATERPILLAR

Mosquitoes bite.
DON'T BELIEVE IT!

 Mosquitoes don't have jaws. They don't have teeth. They can't even open their mouths. In other words—mosquitoes can't bite!

A female mosquito lands on someone's skin. Out pop six small, sharp needles. These needles are called stylets. The stylets cut through the skin. Down they go until they hit a blood vessel.

Meanwhile the mosquito drips saliva into the wound. The saliva stops the blood from clotting. The blood flows easily. The mosquito sips as much blood as it needs. When finished, it pulls out the stylets and flies away.

Most people are allergic to the mosquito's saliva. It forms a red, itchy bump on the skin. We call it a "mosquito bite." But it's not a bite at all!

Moths eat holes in woolen clothes.
DON'T BELIEVE IT!

Some moths live only a few days or weeks. These moths never eat. Other moths live longer. They feed on fruit juices and flower nectar. But neither kind eats holes in woolen clothes.

Some female moths lay their eggs on woolen clothes. When the eggs hatch, caterpillars crawl out. They eat what is nearby. Perhaps it's your favorite wool sweater or gloves. The nibbles make little holes. Some people call them "moth holes." "Caterpillar holes" would be a better name!

Clothes Moth
tinea pellionella

LARVAE

The Barnyard Bunch

A pony is a young horse.
DON'T BELIEVE IT!

Horses come in many different sizes. Thoroughbred, Arabian, Palomino, and Clydesdale are a few kinds of horses. A pony is a different kind of horse. It is not a young horse. A young horse is a colt if it's a male, or a filly if it's a female.

Ponies are much smaller than most other kinds of horses. Full-grown ponies average around 40 inches from hoof to shoulder. Other horses are about 60 inches. Ponies never grow as big as the other kinds of horses.

The best-known pony is the Shetland pony. It is about 45 inches tall. The Shetland is a gentle horse. This pony makes a good pet for riding or for pulling a small cart.

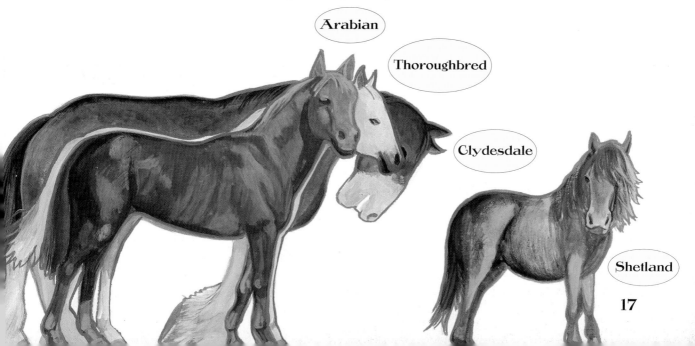

Arabian

Thoroughbred

Clydesdale

Shetland

A hen sits on her eggs.
DON'T BELIEVE IT!

A hen lays an egg almost every day. But she doesn't sit on the egg. It just looks that way.

Each egg begins inside the hen's body. The yolk forms first. Then the egg white and the shell form around the yolk. The shell gets hard as the hen pushes the egg out of her body.

The hen just squats over the egg. She keeps it warm with her soft, downy feathers. If she sat down on the egg, something might happen to it. And you know what!

Pigs are dirty.
DON'T BELIEVE IT!

 If you're like most people, you think pigs are filthy, grubby animals. Well, pigs just don't deserve their bad name.

On farms pigs are often kept in muddy sties. There is a good reason. On hot days, the only way pigs can cool off is by rolling in mud. Pigs use a mud bath the way you use a swim or shower to get comfortable when you're warm.

Mice love cheese.
DON'T BELIEVE IT!

Cheese is not a mouse's favorite food. Mice much prefer nuts, grains, seeds, and fruits. They do eat cheese. But then again, they also eat glue, leather, paste, and soap!

It's a fact. A mouse will eat almost anything. In their search for food, mice gnaw holes in wood and furniture. They tear apart books and clothing.

No one knows where the idea that mice love cheese got started. Probably it began very long ago. People set mousetraps to get rid of these household pests. Maybe they just found it easy to use cheese as the bait.

A rabbit likes to be picked up by its ears.
DON'T BELIEVE IT!

 A rabbit's ears are very sensitive. Picking up a pet rabbit by its ears may seem an easy way to lift it. But it's very painful for the rabbit.

If you want to pick up a rabbit, grasp the loose skin over the rabbit's shoulder. As you raise the rabbit, support its weight with your other hand under the rabbit's body.

Just remember this: Experts say the less a rabbit is carried or petted, the happier it is.

Big and Wild

Elephants drink through their trunks.
DON'T BELIEVE IT!

The elephant's trunk is both its nose and its upper lip. The elephant uses its trunk as an arm and a hand, too. But the trunk is not the elephant's mouth. Its mouth is *under* the trunk.

A thirsty elephant sucks up water with its trunk. It uses the trunk the way you use a straw. But it can't swallow the water this way. It must first curl the trunk and spray the water into its mouth.

The elephant also uses its trunk to reach the plants, roots, and branches it eats. The end of its trunk is like a hand. With it, the elephant can hold and place food in its mouth.

Gorillas are fierce.
DON'T BELIEVE IT!

 Gorillas are around six feet tall and weigh 450 pounds. They have long teeth and can look ferocious. When excited, male gorillas make loud, threatening sounds. But gorillas are not fierce at all.

Actually, gorillas are shy, friendly animals. They live in close, family groups and are devoted to their young. Wild gorillas mostly eat leaves, fruits, and tree bark. They only harm human beings when attacked by them.

Whales do not have hair.
DON'T BELIEVE IT!

Whales are mammals. All mammals have hair or fur. So, too, does the whale. But whales only have a few hairs on the head.

Whales have smooth, rubbery skin. Instead of hair to keep it warm, a whale has a layer of fat called blubber. Several stiff strands of hair grow out from its head. These strands are all that remain from the whale's ancestors.

Long, long ago, the whale ancestors lived on land. They walked on four legs and were covered with fur. Over millions of years, whales lost their legs and their fur. They became more fit for living in the sea than on land.

Mesonychid
more than 50 million years ago

29

Giraffes have more neck bones than humans do.
DON'T BELIEVE IT!

A giraffe has the longest neck of any animal. It is around 11 feet long! A human's neck is no more than a few inches long. But both giraffes and humans have the same number of bones in their necks.

Humans and giraffes each have exactly seven neck bones. Even whales, which don't have necks, have the same seven bones! But there is one big difference between humans and giraffes. Giraffes have much longer bones than humans do. The longer bones make a giraffe's neck long enough to reach the treetops.

A camel's hump is filled with water.
DON'T BELIEVE IT!

 A camel's hump is a big glob of fat—not water! Most animals and people have fat spread all over the body. Not the camel. It keeps most of its fat in one place. In fact, the hump usually holds over 80 pounds of fat!

The camel produces water from the fat in its hump. Many camels live in deserts where there is very little water. Thanks to the hump, the camel can go about eight days in summer without having a drop to drink. In winter, a camel can hold out for as long as eight weeks.

The big, fatty hump also comes in handy when supplies of food run out. In the desert, the camel cannot always find the leaves, seeds, and twigs it usually eats to stay alive. Then it gets food from the stored fat in its hump.

Bears hibernate all winter.
DON'T BELIEVE IT!

 Bats and badgers, snakes and snails, frogs and toads, and several other animals go into a deep sleep for the winter months. We say that they hibernate. Their bodies become cold, stiff, and unmoving. Their temperature drops. Their hearts beat more slowly. They breathe less often. They do not eat. And they can't be wakened until the spring.

Bears don't hibernate. They do go to sleep for a long time when winter comes. But their body temperature does not go very low. They can easily be awakened. Female bears even give birth to their cubs during the winter.

On warm winter days, the bears awaken. They leave their caves and look for food. Then they go back to sleep. Yes, bears sleep for most of the winter. But no, they don't hibernate.

Wolves attack people.
DON'T BELIEVE IT!

Do you know the story of "The Three Little Pigs" and the big, bad wolf? How about "Little Red Riding Hood"? Most of us do. From the time we are little, we hear tales that make us afraid of wolves.

But real wolves are shy around people and rarely harm them. Wolves survive by hunting and eating wild animals. Sometimes the wolves can't find enough moose, deer, or rabbits. Then the wolves may attack sheep, cattle, and other farm animals.

Old tales about wolves made people feel that it was all right to kill wolves. Today most of the wolves in the United States are gone.

Small and Wild

Squirrels remember where they hide nuts.
DON'T BELIEVE IT!

Squirrels bury nuts every fall. That's a fact! But do you know what happens to those nuts in the winter?

Scientists tell us that the squirrels soon forget where they hid the nuts. By the winter they can almost never find the nuts they buried!

Squirrels have a very good sense of smell. They sniff around for hidden nuts. Most of the time, the nuts they find are not the ones they buried. But they do find nuts that others "squirreled away." These nuts taste just as good as their own!

Touching a toad causes warts.
DON'T BELIEVE IT!

 Toads are small animals that look like frogs. Most toads have dry skin covered with bumps. The bumps look like warts. Warts are hard, rough growths that some people get on their skin. But the toad's bumps are not warts.

Warts are caused by a virus, which is a kind of germ. We do not know how the virus gets onto someone's skin. But it does not come from toads.

Still, you should not touch toads. Toads have a poison on their skin to keep away their enemies. Touching a toad may hurt your skin.

Poisonous Fire-Bellied Toad
Bombina Orientalis

Porcupines shoot quills at their enemies.
DON'T BELIEVE IT!

A porcupine's back, sides, and tail are covered with strong, stiff, pointed hairs called quills. The quills protect the porcupine from danger. Porcupines don't have to "shoot" quills at their enemies.

To warn off attackers, the porcupine shakes its short, quill-tipped tail. This makes a loud rattling noise. Most intruders take the hint. They run away. If not, the porcupine swings its tail or backs into the attacker with its quills.

The quills easily come loose from the porcupine's skin. (Later, the porcupine grows new ones.) The quills that get stuck in the victim's skin begin to hurt. Sharp barbs make the quills very hard to pull out. They sometimes remain in the enemy until it dies.

Hedgehogs are porcupines.
DON'T BELIEVE IT!

Hedgehogs and porcupines look alike. Both have short legs and a long snout. Both are covered with long, sharp quills or spines. Sometimes porcupines in America are called hedgehogs. But hedgehogs and porcupines are very different animals.

Hedgehogs live only in Asia, Africa, and Europe. Porcupines are also found in North and South America. Hedgehogs are about nine inches long and weigh two pounds. Porcupines are three feet long and weigh 20 pounds.

Hedgehogs mostly eat insects, snakes, and birds. Porcupines prefer pine needles and bark. When attacked, hedgehogs roll into balls with the spines sticking out. Porcupines fight back by striking at the enemy with their quills.

North American Porcupine
Erethizion dorsatum

White-bellied Hedgehog
Atelerix Albiventris

Long-eared Hedgehog
Hemiechinus auritus

Prehensile-tailed Porcupine
Coendon prehensilis

Great-crested Porcupine
Hystrix Cristata

South-African Hedgehog
Atelerix Frontalis

A prairie dog is a kind of dog.
DON'T BELIEVE IT!

The prairie dog got its name from the harsh noise it sometimes makes. The sound is like a dog's bark. But prairie dogs are not related to dogs. Their closest relative is the squirrel!

Prairie dogs live on the grasslands of North America. They live in burrows under the ground at night. During the day they come out to feed on grass and insects. Each prairie dog burrow is home to perhaps 500 animals.

Carnival of Cats

Lions and tigers live in the jungles of Africa.

DON'T BELIEVE IT!

 First of all, there are no tigers in Africa. Wild tigers today are found only in Asia. Tigers did live in Africa hundreds of years ago. But those animals are now extinct. Even in Asia not many are left.

Second, few lions make their home in jungles. Most live and hunt on Africa's grassy plains.

Bengal
panthera tigris tigris
BANGLADESH, BHUTAN,
INDIA, NEPAL
3,030 left

Lion
panthera leo
AFRICA AND INDIA
about 21,000 left

Siberian
panthera tigris altaica
CHINA, KOREA, RUSSIA
150 left

Amoy
panthera tigris amoyensis
SOUTH CHINA
less than 50 left

IndoChina
panthera tigris corbetti
CAMBODIA, LAOS, MALAYSIA,
MYANMAR, THAILAND, VIETNAM
1,000 left

Java
panthera tigris sondaica
JAVA
Extinct, 1980's

Caspian
panthera tigris virgata
AFGHANISTAN, IRAN,
TURKESTAN, TURKEY
Extinct, 1970's

Sumatra
panthera tigris sumatrae
SUMATRA
400 left

Bali
panthera tigris balica
BALI
Extinct, 1940's

43

You can escape a lion by climbing a tree.
DON'T BELIEVE IT!

There are few trees on the plains of Africa. But this does not mean that lions can't climb trees. In fact, male lions like to climb trees. They often take a nap draped over the branches.

Lions probably climb trees to get away from the heat and flies on the ground—or to chase their prey. Some have been spotted as high as 30 feet up in a tree. So—don't plan to escape a lion by climbing a tree!

The lion is the King of Beasts.
DON'T BELIEVE IT!

 Many people call the male lion the "King of Beasts" for its size, strength, and killer instinct. This splendid-looking animal has a mane that makes it look even bigger than it is.

But male lions are not the greatest hunters. They usually leave the chase to the female lions. And the lioness hunters only catch their prey once for every four times they try!

Experts say that even hyenas are better hunters than lions. In one study, four out of every five animals eaten by lions were actually killed by hyenas.

Among the big cats, the tiger is bigger, the cheetah is faster, and the leopard is stronger than the lion. The lion may not be the King of Beasts. But at least it is the Royal Prince!

BIGGER

STRONGER

FASTER

A panther is a kind of wild animal.
DON'T BELIEVE IT!

 A panther is not any particular kind of animal. It is almost any large cat that is black in color.

Many so-called panthers are really leopards. Leopards generally have tan coats and black spots. But there are some leopards with *black* coats and black spots. They seem all black. People call them panthers.

Jaguars are also big cats. They live in Central and South America. Most have a yellow-brown coat. But some are all black. These animals are also known as panthers.

Mountain lions mostly live in the western part of the United States and Canada. They look like small female African lions. Sometimes they are called pumas or cougars. A few mountain lions live in the eastern United States. They look like their western cousins. What are the eastern mountain lions called? You guessed it. Panthers.

A cat has nine lives.
DON'T BELIEVE IT!

 Have you ever seen a cat
- jump from a high shelf and land gracefully on its feet?
- run along the top of a fence without falling?
- dart and twist to get away from danger?

Cats have amazing reflexes. They don't stop to think how to save themselves. It happens automatically. A cat can usually escape any danger.

Long ago, people wondered why they rarely saw a cat get hurt or killed. "Cats have nine lives!" they said.

Of course, cats don't have nine lives! It just seems that way. Cats are very good at protecting themselves. But they die after just one life—like every other living being.

Creepers and Crawlers

Snakes are wet and slimy.
DON'T BELIEVE IT!

 A snake's body is covered with dry, fishlike scales. Sometimes the scales are smooth. Sometimes the scales have bumps. But the scales are never wet or slimy.

The scales overlap and can stretch apart. That lets a snake bend into any position. A snake can even coil up into a ball!

A few times a year, the snake's skin gets worn. When that happens, the snake crawls out of the old skin. A new skin grows in its place. The change is called molting.

A cobra dances to a snake charmer's music.

DON'T BELIEVE IT!

You can still find snake charmers in India. Each one has a cobra in a basket. The snake charmer plays a flute-like instrument. The cobra rises up in the basket. The snake appears to sway and dance to the music. But snakes are nearly deaf. They cannot hear the music. What's going on here?

When frightened, a cobra lifts up the front part of its body. That's why it coils up out of the basket. The snake sees the snake charmer swaying from side to side. This might be an enemy. The cobra is on guard. It moves from side to side to be ready to strike at the moving figure. The swaying makes it look as though the cobra is dancing!

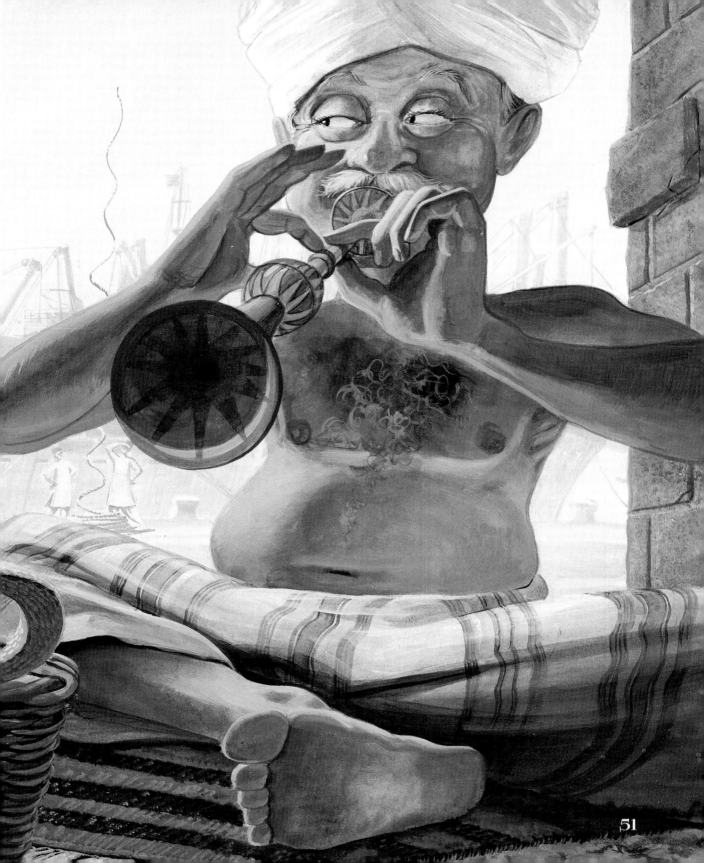

All spiders spin webs.
DON'T BELIEVE IT!

 Most spiders spin webs. But some do not. The tarantula, the biggest spider of them all, doesn't spin a web. One kind builds a little hill of twigs and grass. It sits on top waiting for an insect to come along. As soon as the tarantula spots its victim, it pounces on the unlucky bug.

The bola spider does not make a web, either. But it does spin a single line of silk with a sticky ball at the end. When an insect flies near, the spider flings out the line and traps the insect on the sticky ball.

A spider is an insect.
DON'T BELIEVE IT!

 Spiders are not insects like flies, ants, bees, or moths.

Here's why:

Insects have six legs. Spiders have eight.

The insect body is divided into three parts. The spider body has only two.

Most insects have wings. Spiders do not have wings.

Most insects have feelers, or antennae. Spiders do not have antennae.

Most insects hunt their food. Most spiders wait for prey to get caught in their webs.

Spiders belong to a group of small animals called arachnids (uh-RAK-nids). Other members of this group are ticks, mites, and scorpions.

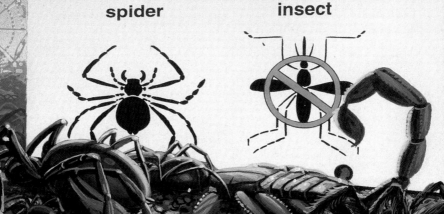

Spiderworld!
WHERE ARACHNIDS ARE KING!
NO INSECTS
spider   insect

A daddy longlegs is a spider.
DON'T BELIEVE IT!

The daddy longlegs is an arachnid like the spider. But it's not a spider. Spiders and daddy longlegs are the same in a couple of ways. Both have eight legs. And both have neither wings nor antennae.

But they are different in a few ways. The daddy longlegs' body has one part, not two parts like the spider. It doesn't bite. And when disturbed, the daddy longlegs sometimes gives off an awful smell.

A silkworm is a worm.
DON'T BELIEVE IT!

 Everyone knows that a silkworm makes silk. But did you know that a silkworm is not a worm? It's a caterpillar!

Early every summer female moths lay their eggs. One kind of white moth, *Bombyx mori*, lays up to 500 eggs. When the eggs hatch, caterpillars crawl out.

Each caterpillar eats and eats. It grows very big. In about a month it is three inches long and nearly an inch thick. It really looks like a worm.

Then the caterpillar starts to spin a cocoon. In its body it makes a thread of silk to form the cocoon. When the cocoon is done, the silk farmer heats the cocoon. This kills the caterpillar. Then the farmer unwinds the long silk thread and sends it to a factory. There machines turn the silk into thread.

The farmer only heats some of the cocoons. He leaves the rest alone. In about three weeks a full grown moth comes out of each one. These moths lay the eggs for next year's caterpillars.

Crickets chirp with their legs.
DON'T BELIEVE IT!

Crickets *hear* with their legs. They chirp with their wings! The male crickets rub the sharp, hard edge of one wing against the toothy edge of the other wing. That makes the chirping sound.

Crickets have flat, round spots under the knee joints of their front legs. These spots work just like the eardrums inside your ears. The spots pick up sound waves from the air and send messages to the cricket's brain.

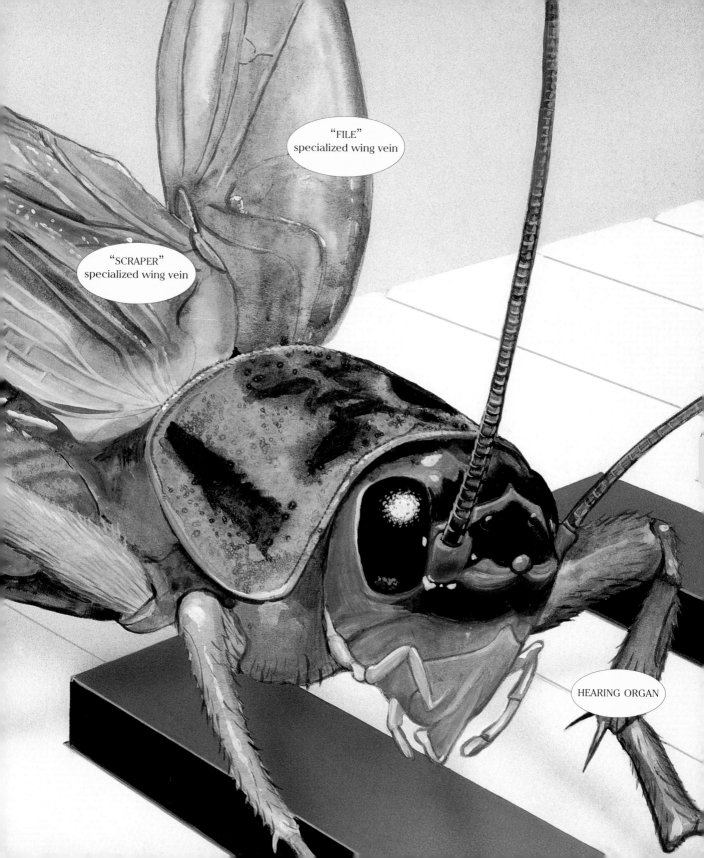

Centipedes have 100 legs.
DON'T BELIEVE IT!

The word centipede means "100 legs." But some kinds of centipede insects have only 30 legs. The biggest species have about 350 legs. All the rest fall in between. Early scientists probably just guessed at the number when they gave them the name "centipede."

Centipedes look like worms or caterpillars. The centipede's body is divided into lots of separate parts. The parts are joined, one behind the other. Each part has a pair of legs. Can you imagine a centipede parade with all of them trying to stay in step?

YOU COUNT'EM
CENTIPEDES
1¢ A SEGMENT

Fishy Facts

Fish drink water.
DON'T BELIEVE IT!

 A fish opens and shuts its mouth as it swims along. It looks as if the fish is gulping water. But fish don't drink the water!

The water just passes over their gills. The fish's gills are two slits on the sides of its head. They are somewhat like our lungs.

As the water passes over the gills, the gills take out the oxygen that is mixed in with the water. With each swish of water, the fish gets another "breath" of oxygen. The water then passes back into the ocean, river, or lake. The water that fish need comes from moisture in the food they eat.

Fish never sleep.
DON'T BELIEVE IT!

 Fish have big bulging eyes. They can see all around. But they do not have eyelids and cannot close their eyes. Then how do they sleep?

Fish sleep with their eyes open. Some rest on the bottom of a sea, river, or lake. They may doze under a covering of sand. Others nap while floating or swimming in the water. If an enemy comes near, though, they sense it. And they quickly rush to escape.

SSSH! DO NOT DISTURB!

Flying fish really fly.
DON'T BELIEVE IT!

 Flying fish leap out of the water at speeds of about 30 miles an hour. But are they flying? No. They are only gliding.

Once the fish leap out of the water, they don't go any higher. The fish fins merely spread out like the wings of an airplane. The wings let the fish soar over the water for up to a quarter mile. Then the fish glides back into the water.

Flying squirrels are gliders, too. Thin skins connect their front and rear legs. The skin is like a parachute that keeps the animals in the air when they jump off a tree.

Flying squirrels in the United States can glide over 100 feet from one tree to the ground or to a lower tree.

Empty crab shells come from dead crabs.
DON'T BELIEVE IT!

 Did you ever find an empty crab shell on a beach? Most people think these shells come from dead crabs. But that's not the story at all.

The shell is the crab's skeleton. The skeleton is on the *outside* of the body. It is different from your skeleton. The bones of your skeleton are *inside* your body.

There is another important difference. The bones of your skeleton get longer and thicker as you grow bigger. But the crab's skeleton doesn't change. It always stays the same. It can't stretch to make more room as the crab grows in size.

So what happens when a crab becomes too big for its skeleton shell? It wriggles out and grows a new, bigger shell. The shells you find on the beach come from live crabs. They are left behind when the crabs grow new shells!